The Boy in the Stars

Written by Devon Peek

Illustrated by Kirsty Oxley

For Darcie and Dax

People always talk of the man on the moon,
but never of the boy who was taken too soon.
Taken from his mum, his dad, his sister too.
He was far more special than anyone knew.

Who is the boy in the stars and what does he do?
What makes him different from me and you?
His name is Dax, he's two years old,
with big brown eyes and hair like gold.
So kind and caring, he shines so bright,
whilst up in the dark black sky at night.

So, how did he get there,
up in the sky?
We'll have to go back to
understand why.

The stars in the sky were growing weary and weak,
their beautiful sparkles depended on little Dax Peek.

The stars, they realised he was special from the rest,
he had strength and bravery of the very best.
From up high in the sky they saw his light,
invisible to us, but it was glowing so bright.

The stars they were tired, struggling to gleam,
So, they all sent a message through a special beam.
A message for help, an SOS.
Dax had the light to fix their distress.

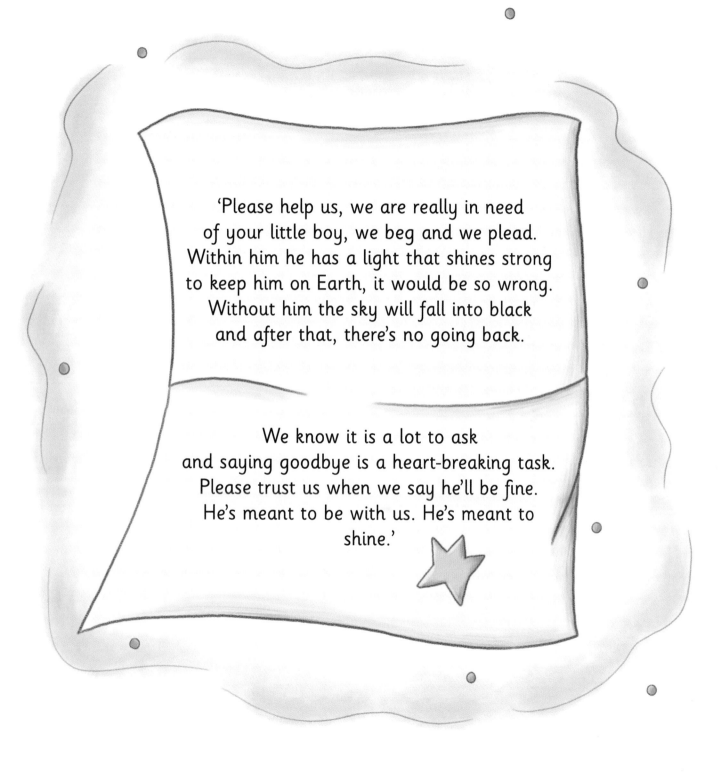

'Please help us, we are really in need
of your little boy, we beg and we plead.
Within him he has a light that shines strong
to keep him on Earth, it would be so wrong.
Without him the sky will fall into black
and after that, there's no going back.

We know it is a lot to ask
and saying goodbye is a heart-breaking task.
Please trust us when we say he'll be fine.
He's meant to be with us. He's meant to
shine.'

His family, they all looked at each other
wondering who wanted Darcie's little brother.
It was then that they saw a small flicker of light,
as a star came closer, they stood in shock at the sight.
It slowly moved closer, in front of them all.
Realisation sunk in and their hearts started to fall.

They didn't want this, they cried and couldn't let go.
They stood sad and confused but Dax seemed to know.
Still dressed in his pjs, it was time to leave.
Leaving his family behind, where they'd forever grieve.

They all hugged and they kissed,
Dax would be so sorely missed.
He let go and took the star in his grasp
as his family let out a tear-filled gasp.
His toy dog still in hand, he held onto her tight.
As both Dax and the star took off into the night.

He's made friends with the stars, lots to meet and explore.
They can't thank him enough, they're not sad anymore.
He tells them stories of adventures he had
back home with his sister, his mum and his dad.
They'll be reunited one day, just not for a while,
until then, he cuddles the stars and he makes them smile.

He jumps round the stars making them glow
and stops to watch the world below.
He looks over his sister, his mum and dad too.
He watches them all from his spectacular view.
The stars, they twinkle and no longer cry.
His light has restored the sparkling night sky.
The stars they adore him, he is their treasure.
But the love of his family, nothing can measure.

He checks that they smile and are doing ok.
Sometimes he sprinkles stardust their way.
He watches the people, the trains and the cars,
it's the most beautiful view from up in the stars.

His family miss him, their hearts still ache.
They can no longer see him when they are awake.
So, instead he draws shapes in the clouds to show
that although they can't see him, he's still there and they know.
He draws all kinds of things - animals, people and love hearts too!
As his family look up to find the shapes that he drew.

When the sun goes down and the sky falls black,
he hears them say "Goodnight" and he twinkles
"Night - night" back.

Night-night!

Goodnight!

So, when you next see the stars from below,
make sure to look up and shout out "Hello!".
Give him a big smile and give him a wave,
remember the light that little Dax gave.
He can see you and hear the words that you say,
and it means so much that he's remembered each day.

He's up there in the starry sky that you look at.
His bravery and strength, we must not forget that.

Printed in Great Britain
by Amazon

69666312R00015